MY FRIEND FANG

and other GREAT STORIES for kids

Learning how to be someone who has good friends.

JERRY D. THOMAS

Pacific Press® Publishing Association
Nampa, Idaho
Oshawa, Ontario, Canada

Editor: Aileen Andres Sox
Designer: Robert N. Mason
Illustration/Art Direction: Justinen Creative Group
Cover Layout: Dennis Ferree
Typeset in Century Old Style 13/17

Great Stories Magabook Copyright © 2001 by
Pacific Press® Publishing Association
Printed in the United States of America
All Rights Reserved

ISBN 0-8163-1822-0

01 02 03 04 05 • 5 4 3 2 1

Contents

New Kid in the Fort

1

Shhh!" Manny whispered. "Keep your head down."

Jake ducked and barely breathed. Between the green leaves on the tree's branches, he could see the turning wheels of two bicycles.

Manny whispered again. "A couple of teenagers rode through here last week on their dirt bikes and tore up my old fort. Glad I wasn't here—they like to chase kids around the woods on their bikes."

Jake's eyes got big, but he didn't say anything. Even though he couldn't see the riders' faces, he could hear their voices.

"This is really nice," one person said. "I never knew these woods were here."

"Oh yeah," the other replied, "these woods were here before this town was. I grew up around here. Back then, kids used to build forts and play games all through the trees. But I guess the only thing kids do now is watch TV or play computer games."

Dealing with prejudice; kindness to animals

Manny snickered behind his hand as the bikes disappeared around a turn in the trail. "I knew they wouldn't see us."

"Zowie!" Jake said. "This is a great fort. How did you find it?"

"I was following a rabbit through the bushes, and it led me here. There was kind of a shallow dip here behind the log, so I filled it with leaves. Now, it's cozy, and no one can find me."

"Do you play here a lot?"

Manny's eyes twinkled. "All the time. See that big fir tree over there?" He pulled a limb back so they could see through the leaves. "That's where Nathan has his new hideout. He doesn't think I know where it is, but I've been hiding here, watching him and his little brother, Brody, for two days."

Jake leaned back against the fallen tree trunk. "This place is way better than my old neighborhood. Boy, am I glad we

New Kid in the Fort

moved here—and just in time for summer!"

A rustling sound in the leaves behind him brought Manny's finger to his lips. Jake twisted around just in time to see a girl's head pop up over the top of the trunk. She had brown hair just like Manny's.

"Manny, come quick! Something happened to Shadow!" the girl said. Then she turned and disappeared. Before Jake could say a word, Manny hopped up and followed her.

Jake joined the chase. "Manny, who was that?" he called after his new friend. "Where are you going? And who is Shadow?"

The girl shouted back over her shoulder. "Stick around. You'll find out. Just hurry!"

Manny didn't stop. He waved his arm. "Come on!"

They raced between tree trunks and bushes, jumped over logs, and almost stopped in front of an enormous briar patch. "There's no way we can run through that," Jake panted.

But the girl didn't wait. She dropped down on her hands

and knees and crawled into the briars. Manny followed right behind her. Jake shook his head but bent down and saw that they were following a kind of a tunnel through the thorny vines.

"Zowie! I hope these guys know where they're going." Then he plunged in after them.

The vines had been carefully cut, and Jake wasn't poked at all. He popped out the other side and kept going. Before long, he was following Manny and the girl out into someone's back-yard. "Hey, Manny, are you sure this is OK?" he called before his friend disappeared around the corner of a white-and-brown house.

"Come on!" Manny shouted again.

Jake raced to catch up. Under a tree in the yard of a house across the street, a small crowd of kids had gathered. Jake followed Manny and then stood on his tiptoes to see.

There on the ground lay a clump of black-and-white feathers. "What is that?" Jake whispered. Manny didn't answer, but the girl with the brown hair did.

"It's Shadow. He's a magpie."

"A what?"

A kid on the other side of the circle rolled his eyes. "It's a bird. You know, mostly black with white across the wings and tail?"

"Give him a break, Nathan," Manny said. "Jake just moved here. He probably never saw a magpie before. What happened to Shadow?"

A little kid spoke up. "I saw him from my window." He pointed to the house behind him. "He was on the ground, and my cat Fluffy was chasing him."

"So Fluffy caught him and killed him?" Manny asked.

"I ran out as fast as I could," the little kid protested. "I chased Fluffy away and called Anna. Then she went to get you."

Jake knelt down to look at the bird. He could see that one wing was broken and many feathers were missing. "Whose bird is this?" he asked suddenly.

"What do you mean, whose bird?" Nathan asked. "It doesn't belong to anyone. It just hangs around the neighborhood, pestering people and getting into trash. Like Leonard always said, 'Magpies are just pigs with wings.' "

"Yeah," the little boy next to Nathan added, "Leonard said that the only good magpie was a dead one. Right, Nathan?"

Everyone was quiet for a moment. Jake kept examining the still bird. Then Anna spoke up. "I don't care what you or Leonard say, Brody. I like magpies. And I'm going to miss having Shadow follow me around begging for food."

Brody laughed. "I bet Fluffy won't miss him. He used to fly down and eat food from Fluffy's bowl. So Fluffy decided to eat him!"

Suddenly, Jake reached down and scooped the bird up with both hands. "Ugh, gross," Nathan said, as everyone backed away. "Put that dead thing down."

"It's not dead," Jake said. "He's still breathing."

"What? Are you sure?" Everyone closed in again.

Jake turned away. "We have to get him to the vet Manny, is your house near? Will your mom take us?"

Manny pointed back at the white-and-brown house. "We live there. But my mom won't spend any money taking a bird to the vet. She'll say there are lots more where he came from."

Anna nodded, along with most of the other kids. "No one would spend any money saving a magpie," Nathan said.

"Well, my mother will," Jake said. He dashed down the street toward home, holding the bird carefully. He was shouting before he even got to the front door of his house. "Mom! Mom, come quick!"

It only took a minute for Jake's mother to see the problem and grab her purse. As they drove back by, Jake saw that Nathan and Brody and the other kids were still under the tree. But Manny and Anna were across the street in their own yard.

I wonder why Manny hasn't shown Nathan his fort. I wonder if they play together at all. Then the bird stirred in his lap.

"Hurry, Mom. I think he's waking up."

Who Shot Shadow?

D r. Morgan led Jake and his mother into the office after he had spent some time with the bird. "Well, there's good news and bad news," he said.

"The good news is, the magpie will live. And that surprises me. Usually, just the shock of being handled by humans and being held captive will keep a wild bird from recovering from the injury."

"He's kind of a neighborhood pet," Jake explained. "He's been following the kids around since spring, begging for food. He seems to like people."

"That would explain it," Dr. Morgan agreed. "Well, he was mauled by that cat, and he's still in a little shock, but those wounds will heal. He would be fine if someone hadn't shot his wing."

"Shot him? Zowie! Are you sure?"

The vet nodded. "Probably a BB gun. When his wing bone shattered, he fell to the ground. Then the cat caught him."

Dealing with prejudice; kindness to animals

Jake let out a big breath. "What's the bad news?"

Dr. Morgan sighed. "Knowing that he's been kind of a pet to the children makes this even worse. The broken wing will never heal properly, so the bird will never be able to fly again. Even if he is fed by people, he won't be able to survive in the wild. We'll have to put the bird to sleep."

Jake's mouth fell open. "What? You can't do that!"

"Couldn't we take care of it?" Jake's mother asked. "We've raised birds before—parakeets and parrots."

"You have a cage? A big one?"

Jake jumped up and held his hand up as high as his head. "It's this big. We had it for my parrot, Gomez."

Dr. Morgan looked at Jake for a moment. "Usually, I wouldn't recommend that a wild bird be kept by anyone. But this one is used to humans. We can't set him free, so maybe your cage is the best thing for him."

Jake was still beaming as they drove home with Shadow in a box. "Don't forget what Dr. Morgan told you about caring for that bird," his mother said.

"I won't, Mom. I'm sure other kids will help me."

Jake was hosing out the big cage on his porch when Nathan and Brody walked up. "So, where did you bury the magpie?" Brody asked.

Jake blasted the bottom of the cage. "I didn't. Shadow is alive. He's going to be fine. Except for his wing. He won't ever be able to fly again."

Nathan laughed. "Then Fluffy will have him for lunch before long."

"Nope," Jake replied. "That's what this cage is for. I'm keeping Shadow as a pet."

"Why would anyone want a flying pig for a pet?" Nathan

rolled his eyes.

"I like birds," Jake explained. "I used to have some parakeets. And a parrot."

"A parrot would be cool," Nathan said. "Could yours talk?"

Jake shrugged. "He learned to say a few words. Mostly he just squawked. But I liked having him around." He snapped off the water. "There, that's done. Now it's ready for Shadow."

Shadow inspected his new home carefully, walking from corner to corner. Jake put Shadow's food and water dishes in the cage and brought an extra treat for his new pet.

"Hello, Shadow. Hello, boy." Jake held a peanut out to the bird as he talked. Shadow stuck his beak through the bars of the cage and grabbed it. Holding the peanut in one claw, he jabbed at it until the shell cracked.

Nathan and Brody watched for a minute, then got up. "We have to go," Nathan said. "You wanna go out to the woods tomorrow? I'll show you my fort."

"Sure, that would be great." Jake smiled. *Maybe Nathan wants to be friends after all.* Then he heard another voice.

"Hey, Jake!"

Jake looked up to see Manny and Anna at the edge of his yard. "Is Shadow OK?" Anna called.

"Come and see him yourself."

Anna looked at Manny. "Are you sure it's OK?" Manny asked.

Jake waved his arm. "Why wouldn't it be? Come on." They raced across the yard and up the steps.

"Look! He's hopping around and everything!" Anna was delighted to see the bird.

Manny was grinning too. "He looks a little ragged without those feathers. How long until you can let him go?"

Jake frowned. "That's the bad news. His wing was . . . broken, and the vet says Shadow will never be able to fly. But the good news is—he gets to stay with me!"

"You're going to keep him? Right here in this cage?" By the look on Anna's face, Jake knew she liked that idea.

"Will Shadow let you touch him?" Manny asked.

"He lets me touch him," Jake said. "I don't know if he'll let anyone else yet. But he'll take a peanut from your fingers if you hold it out."

They took turns giving Shadow peanuts for a few minutes. Then Jake asked, "Where have you guys been? I thought you'd be waiting when I got back."

"We've had a few problems of our own," Manny said.

"Someone shot a hole in Manny's bedroom window with a BB gun," Anna explained. "We've been trying to figure out who did it."

Jake sat up straight. "Zowie! With a BB gun? Are you sure?"

Manny nodded.

"So who did it?" Jake asked.

"We're not sure," Manny answered. "But I know two kids

on this street who have BB guns."

Jake frowned. "I haven't told anyone else about this, but I think I can trust you two. I know you didn't do it because you were with me."

"Do what?" Manny asked.

"Shadow was shot by a BB gun. That's how his wing was broken. Fluffy must have found him on the ground."

Anna's brown eyes got big. Manny's mouth fell open.

"So," Jake went on, "whoever shot your window must have shot Shadow too. Which kids on the block have a BB gun?"

Manny took a breath. "Carlos has one. He lives in that brick house on the corner. But I haven't seen him around much this summer."

"Nathan has one too," Anna added. "He got it on his birthday last spring. He showed it off to everyone."

I wonder if Nathan did it, Jake thought. *I know he doesn't like magpies—and he doesn't seem to like Manny.* Out loud he said, "Let's not tell anyone about Shadow until we figure out who's doing the shooting."

Who Shot Shadow?

Those Kinds of People

As the summer went by, Jake spent a lot of time with Shadow. Now the bird would follow him around the yard whenever Jake let him out of his cage.

Jake also spent a lot of time playing with Nathan and Manny—but never at the same time. If he was with Manny and Anna, Nathan had other things to do. If he was hanging around with Nathan, Manny never showed up.

One day he was sitting in his yard with Shadow. "Hello, Shadow. Hello," he said as the bird stood on his shoulder.

"Squaak," Shadow answered, begging for more food.

"Hey, Jake," Manny called as he and Anna walked up, "it happened again."

"What happened? Not another magpie hurt, I hope."

"No," Anna answered. "But something else was shot with a BB gun. Our back porch light has a little hole right through it."

Jake frowned. "Zowie. And no one saw who did it, right?

Dealing with prejudice; kindness to animals

Well, we know it wasn't Carlos this time."

"Nope. He's gone to his grandparents' house for the summer," Manny said. "So who did it?"

Anna spoke up. "I still think Nathan is doing it."

"But I told you that he said his mother took away his BB gun for the summer," Jake protested.

"I know," Anna said, "because he got bad grades. But what if he's lying about that, just so we won't suspect him?"

Jake looked at them both. "Why don't you guys ever play with Nathan? You must have had a fight or something. He won't even go near your house—and you never go to his."

"We don't go to any-

18

one's house unless they invite us," Anna said.

"That's true," Jake remembered. "You almost wouldn't come to my house at first. But why? And what's the deal with Nathan?"

Manny shrugged. "He doesn't like us."

"Why?"

Anna answered. "Stick around. You'll find out."

She was right. A few days later, Jake found out without even asking.

He was following Nathan and Brody to their fort. "Hey, aren't we going the long way around?" he asked as they took a different trail through the woods.

"Yeah," Nathan said, "but we go this way to get around that big briar patch behind Manny's house."

Jake was confused. "But there's a path through—"

Brody interrupted him. "We don't go by some people's yards."

"Yeah, I know." Jake was going to ask more, but Nathan stopped and held up his hand. "Did you hear something?" He pointed toward the fort.

"Is it those dirt bikers?" Brody whispered. "C'mon, let's go!"

The three boys crept along as quietly as possible, dodging to stay out of sight of anyone who might be on the bike trail. They heard the roar of a motorcycle, but it could have been far away.

"Good," Nathan said as they got closer to the fort, "we don't have to worry about them today."

They walked near Manny's fort, but Nathan didn't say anything. In fact, with the thick leaves there, he couldn't even see the tree trunk lying on the ground.

But Nathan saw something. Not at Manny's fort—at his. "Oh, great! Look what someone did!"

They raced forward to see that the limbs of the fir tree had been broken or twisted back. Nathan's fort was destroyed. Two books and some pop cans lay scattered on the ground, along with a small hatchet.

"Zowie," Jake said quietly.

"Those dirt-bike jerks!" Brody shouted. "I'd like to—"

"Stop shouting," Nathan commanded. Jake could see that he was steaming mad. "We don't know for sure that those bikers did it. It could have been someone else. Like Manny."

Jake wasn't sure he heard right. "Are you kidding? Manny wouldn't do something like this."

"How would you know?" Nathan demanded. "You've only lived here a few weeks." He picked up the books. "Leonard always said, you just can't trust those people. I guess he was right."

Jake still didn't understand. "Who is this Leonard guy you're always talking about?"

"A kid who used to live in your house—before you moved here," Nathan explained. "He was always telling jokes and making everyone laugh. We used to build forts together and stuff like that."

"And Leonard said you shouldn't trust Manny?"

Nathan bristled. "Hey, Leonard knew a lot of stuff. He was older than me or you."

Jake shook his head. *Maybe this Leonard guy knew something about Manny that I don't know,* he thought. "So, what did Leonard tell you?"

Nathan turned to stare. "Do I have to draw a picture for you? You can't trust Mexicans—people with brown skin and

black hair, like Manny and his family. They're lazy and dumb, and they're liars. You can't trust 'em."

Jake could hardly believe his ears. "That's it? You don't like them because they look different than you? That's crazy!"

"No!" Nathan shouted, "you're the one whose crazy for hanging around with him all the time. He probably tore up my fort because you've been playing with me. So you're going to have to decide—if you play with Mexicans, you're not playing with us."

Jake just stood there while Nathan and Brody picked up their stuff. Shaking his head, he turned to stare at the spot

Those Kinds of People

where the big tree trunk was lying on the ground. *I wonder if Manny is back there right now, listening to this.*
Is there any way Nathan could be right?

Under the Skin

Jake stomped into the house, still upset. "Mom, can I ask you something?"

"Just a minute, Jake. I'm on the phone."

Jake wandered into the kitchen and spread peanut butter on a slice of bread while he waited. His mother came in on the third bite. "So, what's up?"

"Natha dothnt kike Mana becawt—"

"Jake! Finish chewing your food first." She waited until he swallowed.

"Nathan doesn't like Manny because he's a Mexican. He says that all Mexicans are dumb and lazy and that they're liars."

His mom didn't blink. "So, is he right?"

Jake was confused again. "Mom! You're supposed to tell me. I don't know any Mexican people."

"You know Manny," she insisted. "Is he?"

Jake stopped to think. "Manny has the best fort in the woods. He was smart enough to find a great spot and worked

Dealing with prejudice; kindness to animals

hard to make it even better. And he's never lied to me, as far as I know. He and Anna care about Shadow. I like them."

"OK, then," Mom said, "you know Nathan is wrong about Manny. I don't think he's right about other Mexicans, either. Jake, there are some Mexican people who are lazy and some who lie. But there are plenty of people who look like you and me who do the same things."

Jake chewed another bite of his peanut-butter bread. Mom went on. "People are not good or bad because of the color of their skin or the way they look. What matters is what's under

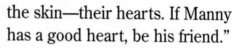

the skin—their hearts. If Manny has a good heart, be his friend."

By the time Jake was through with his snack, he had decided what to do next. He wasn't a bit nervous until he rang the door-bell at the brown-and-white house down the street. "Manny will be glad to see us—right, Shadow?"

"*Squaak,*" Shadow said quietly.

A woman opened the door. "Yes?" she asked, with a puzzled look on her face.

"Hi! I'm Jake. Is Manny home?"

She lifted one eyebrow and almost smiled. "Oh, you are the bird boy, yes?" Then she got serious. "Is there some kind of trouble?"

"No, I just wanted to see if Manny could play," Jake answered.

Her face lighted with a big smile. "Come in! Come in!

Manuel, your friend is here," she called into the next room.

Manny and Anna both rushed in. And they were both surprised to see Jake in their own living room. "What are you

doing here?" Manny asked.

"You came to my house," Jake teased. "Can't I come to yours?"

Manny's answer was a big smile. Anna said, "Anytime—as long as you bring Shadow." She showed the bird off to the rest of the family, then handed him back to Jake when they headed out to the fort.

Shadow squawked as they crawled through the briar patch, but he kept quiet when they tiptoed through the trees and snuck into their fort. Manny took one look through the leaves and hissed, "Hey, what happened to Nathan's fort? Was it those teenage dirt bikers?"

"Nathan thinks it might have been," Jake answered with a

shrug. "They tore it all up."

"I'm glad they didn't find ours," Anna said. "Hey, wait a minute! Manny, didn't we see them on the bike trail last summer, shooting a BB gun?"

"That's right! They're probably the ones who shot you, Shadow."

Jake nodded. "And your house. Come on. Let's make sure they can't find our fort."

They hadn't worked long when Anna's watch alarm beeped. "It's my turn to help my mother with supper," she said. "See you later."

"What're you cooking?" Jake called after her teasingly.

"Stick around. You'll find out."

Not long after Anna left, Jake heard footsteps in the leaves. "Shh!" he hissed. "Someone's coming." They both ducked down and peered through the leaves.

It was Nathan. He was carrying his little hatchet and a rake. He set them down near the bike trail and wandered back and forth, looking at trees and bushes. "He must be looking for a place to build a new fort," Manny whispered.

Sitting there watching Nathan, Jake felt a little weird. *I could be out there helping him,* he thought. Then he argued with himself. *But it's Nathan's fault. He said I couldn't be friends with him and Manny too. And no one's going to tell me who I can be friends with.*

Manny interrupted his thinking. "Do you hear that?" Jake listened, and he heard it too. The sound of motorcycles. And they were getting closer.

A few seconds later, two dirt bikes roared around a curve in the trail. They whipped by Jake and Manny and slid to a stop in front of Nathan.

"Hey, kid," one biker called as the bikes grumbled quietly, "was that your fort we accidently ran into yesterday?" He laughed and twisted the red baseball cap on his head.

"Yeah, you jerks," Nathan answered. He was still mad. "Why don't you leave kids alone?"

"Oh, the little guy's mad," the other biker said. He flipped his ponytail back and forth. "Maybe we should run into something else. Like you." With that, Ponytail released the clutch, and his bike leapt forward, almost onto Nathan's foot.

"Hey, stop it!" Nathan shouted as he backed away. But Red Cap joined in. He roared his bike up beside Nathan and reached out to shove him.

Jake heard Manny mumble something, but he didn't turn. *Come on, Nathan,* he was thinking. *Get away from them!*

Almost as if he had heard Jake's thought, Nathan turned to run. But after only a few steps, he tripped on a root and went sprawling onto the ground.

Jake could just see the bikers riding right over Nathan's body. And laughing. *Zowie! We've got to help Nathan! But how?*

Enemies and Friends

We've got to do something," Jake whispered. But Manny was already doing it. He was running straight at the teenagers. "Pick on someone your own size!" he shouted as he ran up to the one with the ponytail.

"Hey, another one!" Ponytail snorted. "Let's get him!" The back tire sprayed dirt as he took off through the trees after Manny. Red Cap was right behind him.

Jake ran over to Nathan. "Are you OK?"

"I tripped on that root and

Dealing with prejudice; kindness to animals

twisted my ankle," Nathan moaned. "Is Manny crazy? They'll get him for sure."

"Don't be too sure. I think I know where he's headed. Here, hold Shadow. I'm going to help Manny."

Jake raced through the woods after the two bikers. They were closing in on Manny now. Suddenly, Manny went down. "We got him now!" Red Cap shouted.

But Manny hadn't fallen. He dove into the tunnel through the briar patch. Both bikers slammed on their brakes. "Come on. Follow me in here!" Manny taunted them.

Before they could get off their bikes to chase him, Jake ran up behind Red Cap. "Chase someone your own size!" he shouted. Then he turned and ran as fast as he could back toward Manny's fort.

Just from the sound of the motorcycles, he could tell they were chasing him. And getting closer every second. *This plan better work!* he thought. Then he dove through the bushes into the fort.

Hidden under the bushes was the fallen tree trunk. Jake knew that. The bikers didn't.

Crash! Red Cap hit the log. "Oww!" He flew off onto the ground.

Crash! Ponytail hit Red Cap's bike. "Whoa!" He flew on top of Red Cap.

Jake lay still and kept quiet. He hoped Manny and Nathan would do the same.

"Get off me," Red Cap shouted. "Oh, man, look at my bike. My dad's going to kill me. Come on. Let's go."

"But what about those kids?" Ponytail asked.

"Who cares about them? Look at my bike!"

Jake waited until the voices were farther away, then stuck

his head up. "Are you guys OK?" he called.

"No problems here," Manny answered as he came out of the briar patch. "Good trick. They won't be buzzing through these woods for a while."

"I'm OK," Nathan added. "Thanks to you guys."

Jake flopped down near Nathan. "Zowie! That was really something."

"Zowie!"

Jake looked up. Nathan's eyes looked as if they were going to pop out. Manny's mouth was hanging open. "Who said that?" Jake asked. Before anyone could answer, it was said again.

"Zowie! Hello, hello."

"Shadow can talk!" Nathan could hardly believe his ears.

"How did you teach him to do that?" Manny wanted to know.

Jake just laughed. "I wanted to show Nathan that magpies are more than 'pigs with wings.' Then I found out that they're mimics—like crows and jays. And they can be trained to talk. So I've been trying to teach Shadow like I taught my parrot. But this is the first time he ever said anything!"

Nathan looked at the bird as though he had never seen it before. "I can't believe it. A magpie talking! I guess Leonard was wrong."

Then Nathan looked up at Manny. "I guess Leonard was wrong about a lot of things. Thanks for helping me. I didn't deserve it—not after the way I've treated you."

Manny put out his hand and helped Nathan up. "It was nothing. Those two guys couldn't catch a turtle on a race-track. Besides, it was worth it to make a friend."

Just then, the sound of someone crashing through the

trees made them all jump. Jake grabbed Shadow and stood in front of Nathan. But the person who jumped out had a gun!

"Brody! What are you doing?" Nathan pushed past Jake and limped over to his little brother. "And what are you doing with my BB gun?"

Brody was confused. "I heard motorcycles. I thought you might need your gun. Where are those biker guys?"

"Jake and Manny scared them away already," Nathan said. "You know where Mom hid my BB gun?"

"Oh, sure, I found it a long time ago," Brody said. Then he saw Jake and Manny staring at him. "I mean, I found it yesterday."

Nathan saw the stares too. "What's going on?"

Manny cleared his throat. "Someone's been shooting at my house with a BB gun. They broke our porch light and shot a hole in my window."

"It wasn't me," Brody said quickly. "You're just trying to blame someone. It was probably you—or your sister." He turned to Nathan. "You know them. They always lie. The next thing you know, he'll blame me for shooting Shadow."

Jake stopped with a peanut halfway out of his pocket. "Did you say 'shooting Shadow'? Why would you say that?"

Brody hesitated. Nathan butted in. "Shadow wasn't shot. He was hurt by a cat."

"Well, that's not exactly true, Nathan," Jake said. "At the vet's office, I found out that Shadow's wing was broken by a shot from a BB gun. But no one else knows that except Manny, Anna—and the person who shot him."

Brody looked away. "Brody," Nathan asked, "did you do it?"

Brody threw down the gun. "Yes! Yes, I shot Shadow. The only good magpie is a dead one anyway. I want to shoot them all." He turned to Manny. "And I shot your window and porch light too! Everyone knows that Mexicans are liars and cheats. I wish you would all move away, back to where you belong. Right, Nathan?"

Nathan just stared at the ground.

Brody tried again. "Nathan?"

"Brody, Leonard was wrong about some things. He was wrong about a lot of things."

Brody's eyes got watery. "Nathan, you told me about magpies and Mexicans. It's not fair! It's your fault! I'm telling Mom!" Then he turned and ran toward home.

Nathan started to limp after him. "I guess he learned a lot from me—too much. I'd better go explain. See you guys later."

"Zowie," Jake said under his breath.

"Zowie, zowie," Shadow repeated.

Later, Jake was showing off Shadow's talking to the rest of Manny's family when the doorbell rang. Anna opened the door. There stood Nathan.

"Hi! We're having a picnic tomorrow at my house, and I wanted to invite you all to come."

Manny stepped up beside her. "Close your mouth, Anna. You're attracting flies."

Anna was still in shock. "Will someone please tell me what's going on?"

Jake grinned. "Stick around. You'll find out."

"Zowie!" Shadow added.

A Perfect Smile

As soon as she stepped on the Camp Killdeer ski boat, Lindsay knew what she wanted. Even more than she wanted to learn how to ski, she wanted to be just like Nicole.

Lindsay stared as the counselor turned and smiled her perfect smile. *I wish I was as pretty as Nicole. With this job, she must be the most popular girl around,* Lindsay thought.

Nicole was the junior counselor for the Blue Jay cabin and a skiing instructor. *I wish I were in the Blue Jay cabin,* Lindsay thought. *Instead, I'm stuck in the Osprey cabin with Mandy, the kitchen janitor.*

Mandy seemed like a nice person, but she was so . . . plain and boring! Not glamorous and popular like Nicole.

Nicole sat near the front of the boat, her

Influence of older kids; being thoughtful

swimsuit covered by a bright blue Camp Killdeer shirt. When Nicole began rubbing sunscreen on her arms, Lindsay pulled out her bottle and did the same.

"Hey, Nicole," a girl called from the back, "can I borrow your sunscreen? I left mine back at the cabin."

"I don't think so," Nicole called back. "This stuff is expensive." She slipped her sunglasses on and leaned back.

Lindsay put on her sunglasses too.

Nicole showed everyone the basics of skiing, then stayed in the water as each girl took a turn trying.

"Remember, bend your legs and keep your arms straight," Nicole told Amy, one of the girls from the Osprey cabin. "Ready?" She turned to

A Perfect Smile

the driver and said, "Hit it!"

Amy rose up from the water and wobbled along for ten seconds before she fell. "That's a good start," Nicole called. "Who's next?"

Lindsay was the last one to try. Nicole helped her get the skis on her feet. When she was ready, Nicole shouted, "Hit it!" Lindsay tensed up and flopped right over onto her face.

She came up sputtering. "One more time," Nicole said as she helped Lindsay get set again. "Remember to lean back."

It was an instant replay of the first try. When Lindsay popped back up, Nicole was reaching for her skis. "That's enough for one day," she said. "Let's head in."

On the way back, Lindsay found a place near Nicole. "Do you think I'll ever learn?" she asked.

"We'll keep trying," Nicole answered with her perfect smile. "It's really not that hard."

That afternoon, Lindsay went swimming. After a few minutes in the water, she lay down on her towel.

"Hi, Lindsay." Amy and several of the other Ospreys walked up. "We just got here," Amy said. "Can we leave our towels and stuff here while we swim?"

Lindsay tried to imagine what Nicole would say. "I guess so," she answered.

The girls dropped their towels, and Amy opened her bag. "Oh no! I forgot to pack my sunscreen." She looked around. "Lindsay, can I borrow yours?"

Lindsay knew the answer to that one. "I don't think so," she said. "You should have your own. Go buy some at the camp store."

Amy stepped back. "Well, I'm sorry I asked. Come on, girls." With a huff, they gathered their things and stalked away. Lindsay leaned back and practiced her smile.

Later, at the camp store, Lindsay saw a Camp Killdeer shirt like Nicole had. "I'll take this," she told the clerk. *It took almost all my money,* she thought, *but it's worth it.*

When she stepped out of the food line in the cafeteria that night, Lindsay looked around for Nicole.

"The camp shirt looks great on you," someone behind her said. Lindsay whirled around, almost spilling her milk. It was Mandy, wearing a stained apron and holding a mop. "Sorry, I didn't mean to scare you. Can I carry the glass to your table?"

"Uh, thanks," Lindsay stammered. She led the way to a table near the back wall. "See you later." Mandy waved and went back to her mopping.

Nicole sat nearby with a group of junior counselors. She was wearing her blue shirt. Lindsay hoped Nicole would notice that their shirts matched.

She didn't. As she and her friends walked past Lindsay, someone said, "Hey, let's go back down to the beach."

"I don't think so," Nicole answered. "I'm going to wash my hair before campfire."

On the way back to her cabin, Lindsay practiced her new favorite saying. "I don't think so." She tried to sound like Nicole. "I don't think so."

There was talking and laughing in the Osprey cabin as Lindsay walked up. But when she stepped in, it got a lot quieter. *I wonder if they were talking about me,* Lindsay thought. She went quickly to her bunk. *Maybe I'll wash my hair now too.*

She searched through her suitcase. *Oh no! I didn't pack my shampoo. I'll ask someone if I can borrow . . .* She looked

around the cabin. *Maybe I'll just rinse it tonight and buy some shampoo tomorrow.*

She was halfway to the showers before she remembered. *I spent all my money on that blue shirt! Now what will I do?* She trudged on toward the showers, past the Blue Jay cabin.

Maybe Nicole would lend me some shampoo. She walked up to the Blue Jay door but heard voices from inside before she knocked.

"I don't think so. These kids are driving me crazy."

It was Nicole's voice. Lindsay froze and listened.

"They're always whining about something. And clumsy! Some of the kids in my class spent all morning skiing on their faces!"

Lindsay turned and ran from the laughter. With tears in her eyes, she ran past the Osprey cabin to a big tree behind the cafeteria. There she sat, all alone.

"Lindsay? What are you doing here?" It was Mandy, taking out the trash from the kitchen. "Are you OK?"

Lindsay turned her head away. "No, I'm not. I don't have any shampoo. I made all the girls in the cabin mad at me. And people are laughing at me because I can't ski."

Mandy set the trash bags down. "Well, let's see. You can

borrow my shampoo. The other Ospreys are really nice—I know they'll forgive you if you ask. And I'll teach you everything I know about skiing, if you want me to."

Lindsay turned and stared at Mandy. "Why are you being so nice to me?"

Mandy sat down beside her. "Lindsay, the reason I work at this camp is because I like kids. I like to help them learn new things like skiing. I like to help them have fun."

"Really?" Lindsay asked. Mandy's smile told her it was true.

The last day of the week, Lindsay came into the cafeteria. "Mandy! I skied all the way around the lake!"

Mandy smiled. "That's great! I knew you would!"

"Lindsay, come sit with us," Amy called from across the room. Lindsay turned and waved, almost knocking the tray out of a girl's hands.

"I'm sorry," Lindsay said with a perfect smile. "Let me carry your glass for you."

Bird Bingo 7

What bird lays speckled blue eggs?"
Mrs. Watkins's question was barely spoken before
Alex's hand was waving in the air. "Bird bingo!" he
said quickly. Mrs. Watkins walked toward him and bent to
inspect his game card. Alex pointed to the row of four bird
names that he had covered with four kernels of corn.

"Let's see. You have four kernels going right down the
middle of your card. That's the cardinal, the great horned owl,
the osprey, and the robin. Correct. Alex wins again!"

There were groans and smiles around the room as everyone dumped their corn back onto their desks and waited for
the next game. Alex looked over at his friend Matt. Matt whispered, "Way to go! Now you get to pick two prizes from the
Dino-Jar."

Matt looked at the Dino-Jar that sat on the shelf behind
Mrs. Watkins's desk. Its tyrannosaur shape was filled with
neat stuff—like whistles, key chains, cars, combs, and lots of

Kindness; unselfishness

dinosaur-shaped erasers that fit on the end of a pencil. Mrs. Watkins used them to reward kids for being kind to others, for doing excellent work, and for winning classroom games. He knew what he would pick. He needed a green tyrannosaur eraser for his pencil. And a whistle would be just what they needed for the soccer game during recess.

Mrs. Watkins began the next game. "This bird is tall, it can't fly . . ."

Alex found *ostrich* on the left side of his card.

". . . and it lives in New Zealand."

Whoops, Alex thought, *it's not an ostrich. It's a kiwi, but I don't have that on my card.* He noticed that Bobby, sitting in the row next to him, had placed a corn kernel on his card. He did have a kiwi. *I wonder what he would get from the Dino-Jar?* Bobby was smaller than most of the kids in their class. At recess, he was usually the last person picked on a soccer team. *I think everyone likes him,* Alex thought. *They just don't notice him much.*

"This is the only bird that can fly backward," Mrs. Watkins said.

Alex marked *hummingbird* on his card. But he didn't get to mark many others. This time, Mrs. Watkins described birds that weren't on his card. He noticed that Bobby had many of them and was close to winning. Bobby's feet kind of danced around as he sat there, ready for the next clue. Alex smiled. He knew just how it felt to need only one more bird to win. But the next bird was a bald eagle, and Shayna's hand flew up as she said, "Bird Bingo."

"This will be our last game," Mrs. Watkins announced when everyone's corn was back on their desks and they were ready to begin. "It's almost time for recess."

"This time, I'm winning," Matt whispered to Alex.

"I hope so," Alex whispered back. Bobby looked over at both of them and smiled, but he didn't say anything.

"This bird imitates the songs of many other birds," Mrs. Watkins read from her card. Alex quickly covered *mockingbird* with a kernel and saw that Bobby did, too.

"This bird gets its pink color from the shellfish that it eats."

Alex covered *flamingo.* As the game went on, he got closer and closer to winning again. He could see that Matt's card still was nearly empty. But Bobby's was filling up fast.

"This duck often makes its nest in a hollow tree."

Wood duck on Alex's card was quickly covered. Now he only needed one more to win. *What else would I get from the Dino-Jar?* he asked himself. *I know! I saw a key ring in there last week that looked like a silver soccer ball.*

"This large bird can soar for hours over the ocean without flapping its wings."

Albatross, Alex thought. But it wasn't on his card. *It must be on Bobby's, though.* He could see that Bobby's feet were dancing again. *He must be getting close to winning.*

"This bird spends most of its time on the ground and says its own name."

Everyone in the room looked for the same name on their cards—*bobwhite quail*. It was on Alex's card. *I win*, he said to himself. But before his hand went up, he glanced over at Bobby's card. *Just one more, and he would win*, Alex realized.

Alex's hand started up, but he was still looking at Bobby. *He sure would be happy if he won a game. I wonder what he would . . .*

Then Mrs. Watkins spoke again. "This bird is related to the dove. It likes people and buildings and is often found in cities and in parks."

As Alex watched, Bobby's hand shot up. "Bird Bingo!" he shouted. As Mrs. Watkins checked, his feet danced some more.

"Bobby wins," she announced. "You may line up to go out for recess."

Alex looked at Bobby. He had the biggest smile Alex had ever seen on his face. And Alex realized that his own smile was pretty big too.

"You played well today, Alex," Mrs. Watkins said as she walked by his desk. "You know your birds and . . . " She stopped and stared at Alex's card. "Why, Alex, you . . ." Alex looked at Bobby, who was up staring into the Dino-Jar. Mrs. Watkins followed his look. ". . . you should have won again."

She looked at Alex for another second, then said, "All right, class, you are dismissed. Mr. Harkins is waiting for you on the playground. Alex, please come up to my desk."

Matt looked at Alex from across the room. "What happened?" he mouthed, without saying the words.

Alex just shrugged his shoulders. He didn't know what Mrs. Watkins wanted. Was he in trouble for not saying he won? He walked slowly up to her desk.

Mrs. Watkins looked stern sitting behind her desk. "All right, Alex, why don't you tell me what happened. Why didn't you raise your hand when you won the game?"

Alex explained just what happened. "I could see Bobby's

and Matt's cards from my desk. I know it wasn't any of my business to look, but I did. I knew that Bobby only needed one more when Shayna won. When I won again, I could see that he only needed one more again."

"So you didn't raise your hand?"

"Well, I almost did, but then I thought about Bobby, and, you know, he doesn't always do so well in soccer or baseball or anything, and . . ."

Mrs. Watkins interrupted. "And you thought it would be nice if he could win, if he could do something well for a change."

Alex nodded. "But I just barely had time to think about it when you called the next bird, and he did win." He watched to see if she was angry at him. "I promise not to do it again."

"Alex," Mrs. Watkins said, "that was one of the nicest things I've ever seen anyone do. I'm very impressed that you would be so thoughtful and unselfish."

Alex's face broke into a big smile.

"And I know your parents will be impressed, too, when I tell them."

Alex's smile got even bigger.

Mrs. Watkins's smile was pretty big too. "I'm very happy that you are in my class, Alex. Now, you'd better hurry out, or you're going to miss the soccer game."

As he dashed out to the field, Alex said to himself, *I never knew losing a game could make you feel so good.*

"I Hate Him/ I Hate Her"

RACHEL

I knew I didn't like him the first day of school. I told Emily, "Did you see that new kid? He's carrying a briefcase! Can you believe it?"

"Really?" Emily was amazed. "What is he, from another planet?"

Then we found out in homeroom. It wasn't another planet—just another continent. "Class," Mrs. O'Dell announced, "we have a new student this year. Jacob Costanza's family have recently moved back to America from Egypt. His parents were missionaries there.

Being a Christian; dealing with hatred

Now his father is the pastor at Southside Church."

I rolled my eyes at Emily. "Just what we needed," I whispered. "A preacher's kid. No wonder he's so weird."

In case you couldn't tell, I don't like preachers or their kids. In fact, I don't like Christians at all.

JACOB

I thought I would love coming back to America to go to school, but I don't. Everything is so different! I mean, I'm supposed to be an American, but I don't even know what American kids act like.

"Don't worry," Mom said. "You'll fit in fine." Then she sent me off to the first day of school with a briefcase. I thought I would die of embarrassment!

"Mom," I reported that afternoon, "no one in America takes a briefcase to school. They all carry backpacks, or nothing."

"Backpacks?" she asked. "Like they were camping and hiking? How very odd."

"No, Mom, just me. I'm the only one who's odd."

After that first day, it wasn't so bad. In fact, most of the kids are pretty friendly—except for Rachel. She really hates me. And I don't know why. Maybe I should try to be more friendly to her.

RACHEL

I'm going to die! I have never been so embarrassed in my whole life! I was eating lunch in the cafeteria at my usual table, with Emily, when Jacob just walked up and sat down like he belonged there.

"Hi," he said with a toothy smile.

"Hi, Jacob," Emily said.

I said, "Jacob—that's a name from the Bible, right? I guess that's a good name for a preacher's kid." He just took out his lunch. "What's that?" I asked politely.

"It's a kind of Egyptian food," he said. "It's called falafel [fuh-law-ful]."

I wrinkled my nose. "I think I'd call it 'smell-awful.'" Everyone laughed. Even Jacob.

Then smart-mouth Andy said it. "Hey, wasn't the Jacob in the Bible married to Rachel?"

I thought I was going to die. Everyone laughed. Andy couldn't shut up. "Rachel and Jacob. Jacob and Rachel. I guess they're supposed to be together."

"I Hate Him/I Hate Her"

Before they even finished laughing, I had decided two things. The first one was about my name. "Emily," I said later, "from now on, my name is Rach. Don't ever call me Rachel again."

The second thing was this: I'm going to make Jacob wish he had never come back to America.

JACOB

All I did was try to be friendly. I didn't point out that her name was from the Bible too. I even laughed at her stupid joke about my food. But now Rachel really hates me.

I'm getting along fine with the others. Andy picked me to be on his football team at recess. Then he said, "Jacob, grab the football. Let's get to the field before anyone else and practice passing."

So I grabbed the football and ran after him. But as soon as I kicked it, he looked at me like I was crazy. Rachel was right behind us. "Hey, Bible boy," she called, "don't you even know the difference between a football and a soccer ball?"

Then I remembered. "They call soccer 'football' in Egypt. I forgot you meant American football."

Rachel wouldn't let it go. "Well, if you like Egyptian things so much, why don't you go back there. No one wants you here anyway."

I knew she was trying to make me mad. It worked. I threw the football down and stomped away.

I hate Rachel.

RACHEL

"Rach, why do you hate Jacob so much?" Emily asked. "You always call him 'Bible boy' and go out of your way to be mean to him."

I shrugged. "I just do. All those goody-goody Christians make me sick. My mom says no one believes those stories anyway."

"Didn't you used to go to church? Before your parents split up?"

"That's why I hate church," I explained. "My dad always went and acted so perfect. And at home, he would read the Bible to us. Then one day he just left, like he didn't even care about us. If that's what Christians are like, I hate them.

I just know that Jacob is as fake as my father was. And I'm going to make him mad enough to prove that to everyone.

JACOB

"Dad," I asked one night, "is it OK to hate someone who hates you first?"

Dad frowned. "Jacob, the Bible is pretty clear about not hating anyone."

"What if I just don't like someone? What if I don't like them so much I wish they would walk in front of a moving bus?"

"You know," Dad said, "Jesus had to deal with people who hated Him. Do you know what He did and what He taught His followers to do?"

"What?"

"He treated them with kindness. Return good for evil, He told them. That's what being a Christian is all about. Is this person who hates you a Christian?"

"Rachel? She hates Christians. At least, that's what she tells everyone."

Dad thought for a moment. "Then I guess you can show her what a Christian is really like. I'll be praying for you, Jacob."

I think I'd better be praying too.

RACHEL

That Jacob makes me so mad! I poured milk on his lunch. I "accidentally" knocked his books off his desk. I even threw his homework in the trash. But he just smiles and says nothing.

JACOB

God, if Rachel does one more thing to me, I'm going to strangle her! Unless You help me. Please help me return kindness for evil. Amen.

RACHEL

I can't believe it! Mrs. O'Dell can't make me do it, can she?

JACOB

Just when I thought it couldn't get worse, it did!

SOUVENIRS

RACHEL
"You'll be giving reports on countries of the world," Mrs. O'Dell said. As if that wasn't bad enough, she added more. "And you'll be working in groups of three."

I knew she'd let Emily and me work together—we always do. But our other partner was the big shock. Mrs. O'Dell announced it loud and clear. "Our first group will be Emily, Rachel, and Jacob."

I argued with her. I even begged. "Mrs. O'Dell, we can't work with him—he's a boy." I couldn't really tell her that I hate him. "Please give us another girl."

"Nonsense, Rachel," was her only answer. "You'll do fine."

At lunch, Emily was happy. "This will be fun. Jacob's probably the one person in our class who's been to some other countries."

"He'll probably want to do our report on some Bible land," I grumbled.

Being a Christian; faith in the Bible

That afternoon, Mrs. O'Dell gave everyone time to begin working with their partners. Emily and I pulled our desks up by Jacob's. "Look, Bible boy," I said right away, "we're not doing this report on Israel or some other Bible land. Everyone knows those stories aren't real anyway."

I saw his mouth open and close. He almost got mad and shouted at me. Maybe this will work out after all. . . .

JACOB

I wish Rachel would stop calling me "Bible boy."

It's not my fault Mrs. O'Dell put us together. And I didn't say anything about any Bible lands. But when she started saying the Bible stories are made-up, I almost let her have a piece of my mind.

"Mom, what am I going to do?" I asked after school. "Rachel hates me, but I have to do this report with her and Emily."

"Why don't you invite them to come over here after school and work on the report? We have encyclopedias and everything. I could make some cookies."

I guess it's a good idea. Unless Rachel tries to burn down my house or something.

RACHEL

I guess it makes sense. But I don't like it. Emily wanted to do it as soon as Mrs. O'Dell explained the assignment.

"Class, your reports need to tell where the country is, how many people live there, and something about the way they live. I want pictures that show what the people usually wear, what their houses look like, and what kind of land their country is."

"Rach, we've got to do our report on Egypt," Emily said. "No one else can say they lived in a different country. With Jacob, we'll get the best grade in the class."

"I guess you're right," I agreed. "But I don't have to like it—or him."

When we got together for social studies, I let Emily do the talking. "Jacob, why don't we do our report on Egypt? You could probably tell the class a lot of stuff we wouldn't find in an encyclopedia."

You'll never guess what he did. He invited us to his house to work on the report. Both of us!

JACOB

Well, I wouldn't have believed it, but Rachel and Emily came to my house. Mom was great. "More cookies, girls?" she asked. She makes the best oatmeal-raisin cookies.

"Mrs. Costanza," Emily said between bites, "we want to do our report on Egypt, since Jacob lived there."

"Why, that's a fine idea," she agreed. "Jacob, have you shown them your souvenirs?"

So I took them to my room to show off my collection of keepsakes and stuff. Emily started looking before I could even show her.

"What is this?" she asked, holding up an Egyptian flute. I told her. "What's this?" An Egyptian hat, I explained. While I was showing her the Egyptian sculptures and basket, I kept turning my head to keep an eye on Rachel. She was looking at my other stuff, and I didn't want her breaking it or anything.

"Are these Egyptian coins?" Emily asked. Before I could answer, Rachel interrupted.

"Have you really been to all these places?"

RACHEL

I stared at a silver mouse and a picture of Jacob and his mother with Donald Duck. Disneyland, I'm sure. Then there was the little statue of the Washington Monument. And a pic-

ture of him and his dad in front of the Lincoln Memorial. Washington, D.C.

"Are you guys rich?" I asked.

"No. Missionaries just travel a lot."

There were things from Paris and London. But a funny-looking picture caught my eye. "What's this?"

"You're not going to like it," he said. "It's a picture of me and my dad in a cave under Jerusalem. That tunnel leads up to the city. But they wouldn't let us climb it."

I just stared.

"It's from the story in the Bible—where David's men capture the city by climbing up the tunnel."

I knew that story. "It's real? That place is really there? Still?"

"Cool," Emily said, walking over to look. "What are these rocks?"

You won't believe what he said.

JACOB

"You remember the story of David and Goliath?" I asked. "And how David picked up the stones from the stream for his sling?" They nodded. "I went there. To the same valley. These stones are from that same stream."

I thought Rachel was going to faint. Instead, she sat down on my bed. "I can't believe it," was all she said.

We didn't get much done on our report. Rachel was ready to leave. I don't know if that's good or not.

I hope I did the right thing, telling her that Bible stuff.

RACHEL

"You don't think Jacob was just making up that stuff about the Bible stories, do you?" I asked Emily.

"Rach, do you think he was making up the stuff about Disneyland? Or Washington, D.C.?"

She's right. Of course, he's not. But that means the stories in the Bible are real. And that Jacob is a real Christian. Look at all the mean things I've done to him! And he's always been nice.

Maybe Christians aren't as bad as I thought. I'd better talk to Mom about this.

JACOB

Wow! Something sure changed. Rachel was actually nice to me today. I wonder what that means?

RACHEL

I surprised Emily at lunchtime. I said, "Let's sit with Jacob."

She looked at me. "Rach, what's going on? Are you feeling OK?"

"I'm feeling fine," I told her. "And, Emily—call me Rachel."

No Friends Again

This year is going to be different, Chelley promised herself as she walked up the stairway to her first class. *This year, I'm going to make friends.* After walking up three flights, she checked her notebook to be sure she knew the right room number. "Three fifteen," she mumbled. Then she walked to the door with that number over it.

The first thing she did was bump into a tall red-haired girl. "Sorry," Chelley mumbled, staring at the floor.

The girl shook her head. "My fault. I guess I look like a door," she called over her shoulder to the other kids. They all laughed. Chelley slunk over to an empty desk and tried to disappear.

"All right, let's settle down," the teacher said as she walked in. "My name is Mrs. Yount, and this is your homeroom. This is where you will come first every morning, and I'll be your teacher for science and social studies. Now, let's see who's here. Please tell me if I pronounce your name wrong."

Shyness; making friends;
being an example

Chelley slumped down farther. *Oh, please get it right!* she said silently to the teacher. Before long, the teacher reached her name. "Chelley?" she said as if it started with the same sound as *church*.

Chelley turned red. "It's pronounced Shelley."

Mrs. Yount looked at her with a smile. "Chelley," she said correctly. "OK. Andrea?"

"Here," the red-haired girl answered. "Is it time for recess yet?" Everyone laughed, and Mrs. Yount smiled.

"Not yet," she answered. "Chris?" There was no answer. "Chris?" she asked again. Finally, a boy near the back spun around in his seat.

"Here!" he almost shouted. Everyone laughed again. "Sorry," he mumbled.

"Please stop talking and pay attention, Chris," Mrs. Yount said. "Steven?"

The boy right behind Chris waved his hand. "Here," he called. "I'm here, Mrs. Yount. And I'm paying attention." Everyone laughed except Chris.

"Hey, Steven was the one talking to me," he protested.

Mrs. Yount just said, "Today, you have chosen where you want to sit. If necessary, I'll choose a different seat for you." Then she went on calling the role.

Why can't you be loud and friendly like those kids? Chelley said to herself. *Everyone will want to be friends with Andrea and Chris and Steven.* But Chelley knew she couldn't. If she tried to say something funny, it would sound dumb. And everyone would stare at her like she should be in a cage at the zoo.

"I'd like to introduce one other member of our class," Mrs. Yount said as she finished. She walked to the side of the classroom by the windows. "This is Morey. He's our class hamster."

"Ahh," Chelley moaned. She loved animals. *He looks soft like Benjamin,* she thought, comparing him to her pet rabbit. *I wonder if I can help take care of him.*

Mrs. Yount answered her question. "We'll all take turns taking care of Morey. Each day, one member of the class will be assigned to give him his food and water."

Andrea raised her hand and waved. "Mrs. Yount, can I take care of him first?"

"May I, Andrea," Mrs. Yount said. "May I take care of him."

Andrea looked confused. "You're the teacher. You can take care of him if you want to."

Chelley understood. She almost turned red just thinking about how embarrassed she would be to make that mistake. As she looked around, Chelley looked at a girl who had answered to the name of Caitlin. Caitlin's eyebrows went up. She understood it too.

Mrs. Yount explained. "Andrea, you should say, 'May I take care of Morey,' not 'Can I.' You're asking permission, not asking if you are able. And yes, Andrea, you may."

Chelley turned to see what color Andrea was turning. Everyone was staring. And laughing. But Andrea was laughing too. *She's not even embarrassed! I would have died! I must*

be the Red Face Champion of the World.

As Mrs. Yount gave them their first assignment, Chelley looked over at Caitlin again. *She seems like a friendly person. I wish I could make friends with her.* But inside, Chelley knew it wouldn't happen. This year was going to be just like all those years at her old school.

That next morning, Chelley almost tripped over two suitcases by the front door. "Hey, who's moving out?" she called.

"It's me," her dad answered from the kitchen. "But I'm not moving. I'm leaving on another business trip this morning."

Chelley came and leaned over his shoulder to look at his newspaper. "What do you do on all these trips, Dad?"

He reached up and patted her head. "You know I sell computer programs. I'm traveling to meet with someone who might want to buy some."

Chelley shuddered. "I couldn't do your job—traveling around talking to strangers—I just couldn't."

"It's not so bad, Chelley. They aren't strangers for long. I try to turn them into friends."

"How do you do that so fast, Dad?"

He turned another page of his newspaper as he answered. "It's

No Friends Again

pretty simple, really. You just get them to talk about them-selves. Almost everyone likes to talk about their families or their business—anything about themselves. By paying attention when they talk and not interrupting, you make them feel special and important."

Chelley raised one eyebrow. "And that works?"

"Hey," her dad answered, "that's what's paying for this house. I make friends like that. Then I make money by selling them the things they need."

Chelley hugged him. "You're the greatest," she said. "The greatest salesman—and the greatest dad."

"OK, OK," he said, finally unwrapping from her arms. "Let me finish reading the basketball scores."

"Dad," Chelley protested, "you don't even like basketball."

"No," he admitted, "but my customer tomorrow does. And this will give me another thing to talk to him about. Hey, you'd better get going, or you'll miss your bus."

She hugged him again. "I'll miss you."

"Not for long. I'll be back tomorrow night. Have a good day at school, sweetheart."

On the way to school, Chelley

kept thinking. *I wonder if I could use Dad's tricks to make friends with Caitlin?* But when she got to her classroom, the thought disappeared.

Even before she got to the door, she could hear kids shouting and laughing. Then she heard a voice. "Shh! I think she's coming!"

As Chelley stepped up to the classroom door, everyone was silent.

Shouting Silently

11

Chelley fought the urge to turn and run back down the stairs. She leaned forward and poked her head in the room.

"That's not Mrs. Yount, you chicken," Chris called. He and Steven ran to the front of the room and bent down behind the teacher's desk.

With everyone ignoring her, Chelley walked happily and quickly to her desk. She heard Andrea's voice. "Mrs. Yount is going to have a fit when she sits down. And if she falls over, you guys are going straight to the principal's office."

From listening, Chelley learned that Chris and Steven were unscrewing one of the rollers on Mrs. Yount's chair. Caitlin was shaking

Shyness; making friends; being an example

her head. "What if she falls over and gets hurt?" she asked someone sitting next to her.

Chelley didn't like it either. *Someone should tell Mrs. Yount,* she decided. But when the teacher came in, Chelley was quiet along with everyone else. *Don't sit down!* she shouted silently. But Mrs. Yount did.

Almost. At the last minute, she reached down to roll the chair farther from the desk. With a loud *clunk*, it tipped up. Everyone was even quieter as she looked up. "It seems that a wheel has fallen off my chair," she said finally. "Can I have two volunteers to put it back on? How about you, Chris? And Steven? Thank you."

The rest of the class time went by quietly until Mrs. Yount announced a science project. "As we study gravity and motion, we are going to have a contest. I'm going to divide our class into teams of two. And I want each team to drop a fresh egg from our classroom window and have it fall to the ground without breaking."

The whole class started buzzing. "You can't do that! It's impossible. You couldn't throw a rock from there without breaking it."

"Now, wait a minute," Mrs. Yount interrupted. "I want you to find a way to counteract the force of gravity. Give your egg a parachute. Build a cushion around it. Do whatever you think will keep it from breaking. Next week at this time, we'll be throwing our eggs out the window."

To Chelley's delight, Mrs. Yount assigned her and Caitlin as partners. They moved their desks together. "Hi," Caitlin said. "Do you really think it's possible to keep our egg from breaking?"

Chelley hesitated. "I guess it must be. Mrs. Yount thinks it will work." She could feel her face getting hot. *What did Dad say he did?* Then she remembered. "Have you lived here a long time? My family just moved to this school district."

Caitlin nodded. "I've lived near here since I was born. I went to school with most of these kids last year." She thought for a second. "But my sister went here two years ago. She had Mrs. Yount. Maybe she remembers how they did the egg thing. I'll ask her tonight."

Chelley beamed and tried to remember what to do next.

"Do you have just one sister?" she asked as they opened their science books. Then she listened as Caitlin talked about her sisters and her home on a ranch. When science was over, Chelley knew more about Caitlin than she did about gravity and motion. But that didn't bother her.

Maybe I can really make a friend, Chelley thought as she walked home from the bus stop. *What else did Dad say he does?* As soon as she walked in the door, she called, "Dad! Dad, are you home?"

Her mother stuck her head into the room. "He left on his

trip this morning, remember?"

"Oh yeah." Then Chelley remembered something else. "Mom, don't we have a book about horses?"

Her mother sounded surprised. "Horses? What is it, a report you have to do? I know you don't like horses."

"Mom! It's not for me. It's for a friend—I hope."

Later that week, Chelley hesitated at the door to her class-room. The buzzing sound of kids talking fast and loud almost frightened her. But as she stepped in, no one paid any attention. She was relieved that Chris and Steven weren't doing anything to Mrs. Yount's desk.

But several boys, including those two, were huddled around the hamster cage. While Chelley watched, Andrea ran back to where they were.

"I wonder what they're up to now," Caitlin called from her desk. "Some dumb trick, probably. Hey, Andrea, what are they going to do?"

Chelley listened as Andrea came up to Caitlin's desk. "They're planning another trick on Mrs. Yount," Andrea reported. "When we pack up our eggs and drop them out the window, Mrs. Yount is going to be down on the ground to see if they broke."

"Right," Caitlin agreed. "One of us has to drop the egg, and the other has to be down with Mrs. Yount. So?"

"Well, Chris and Steven are building a parachute to float their egg down. Only they're not going to drop an egg— they're going to hook the hamster up to their parachute!"

Chelly gasped. *They can't do that!* she shouted silently.

Caitlin was thinking the same thing. "Hey, what if Morey gets hurt?"

Andrea shrugged. "You know those two—if they think it'll be funny and shock the teacher, they'll do it. They just want to see her face when she sees little Morey come sailing down."

Just then, Mrs. Yount walked in. "All right, students, let's find our seats," she said.

Just the idea of the poor little hamster being thrown out the window made Chelley too mad to think. Almost before she knew it, she turned to Mrs. Yount and raised her hand.

"Stop It"

12

The sudden silence in the room told Chelley that everyone was staring at her. With her face hot enough to glow in the dark, she tried to slide down out of sight. But Mrs. Yount had already seen her.

"Yes, Chelley?"

"Uh, I, uh." Chelley stared at the floor as she stammered. "I just wondered if we're going to be working on our science projects today."

"Yes, we are," Mrs. Yount answered. "Right after social studies. Now, if everyone will take out their social studies books, we'll get started."

When they did get together for science, Caitlin whispered, "For a second, I thought you were going to tell Mrs. Yount about Chris and Steven's plan."

Chelley shook her head. "I wanted to, but I got embarrassed. I just get really nervous when everyone is looking at me."

Shyness; making friends; being an example

"I'll say you do," Caitlin agreed. "You should see how red your face gets. See, you're getting red again. But don't worry. I always say I'm going to tell on those two myself, but I don't. I guess I'm afraid that everyone will be mad at me. Or that Chris and Steven will start playing tricks on me."

Chelley was amazed. "You're afraid everyone will be mad at you? But everyone likes you!"

"No," Caitlin said with a laugh, "everyone likes Andrea. If she gets mad at you, no one will be your friend."

"Why?" Chelley asked. "What makes her so special?"

Caitlin shrugged. "That's just the way the kids here think. Who knows why? I don't worry about it much. Whether I have friends here or not, I still have my horse. And my sister is going to teach me how to barrel-race."

Chelley smiled. "So, you have a quarter horse."

Caitlin looked surprised. "How did you know that?"

"I know that most people who do barrel racing at rodeos

use quarter horses," Chelley answered.

Caitlin was impressed. "You know a lot about horses for someone who lives in the city. Did you ever own one?"

"No. I'm just interested." Chelley's smile froze when Mrs. Yount stepped up.

"Girls, unless you're planning to drop horses out of the window, I suggest you get busy with your science project."

"Yes, ma'am," Caitlin said. Chelley just turned red. "I got an idea last night," Caitlin went on. "My sister said that a lot of people in her class wrapped their eggs in a big ball of cloth or paper. I saw an old flat basketball in our garage. What if we cut it open, stuff it full of soft paper or cloth, and put the egg in the middle?"

"Good idea," Chelley agreed. "If we tape it well, it won't pop open when it hits the ground. And the egg should be safe with that much padding. When can we put it together?"

Caitlin chewed on her pencil. "We really should practice it once to see if the egg breaks. Hey, why don't you come to my house after school? I'll get an egg from my mom, and we'll throw the basketball from the barn loft."

Chelley grinned. "I'll call my mother at lunchtime."

When she walked through the door that evening, Chelley was still grinning. "Mom! I'm home!"

Mom appeared with the phone stuck to her ear. "I'm talking to your father. He wants to know if you had a good time."

"Tell him Yes," Chelley answered. "Oh, and tell him thanks for helping me make a friend." As she walked to the refrigerator, Chelley heard her mother's voice.

"I don't know why she said that. Ask her when you get home."

Chelley grabbed two carrots and headed to the backyard.

"Hi, Benjamin," she said as she stuck one carrot through her rabbit's cage. One wiggle of his nose led to some serious chomping. With her own carrot between her teeth, Chelley opened the cage and brought her pet out to sit on her lap.

"I sure had fun today, Benjamin," she said as they both crunched another bite. "Our basketball egg didn't break, and we spent most of the afternoon playing around the barn and with Caitlin's horse."

Benjamin paused between bites. "Don't worry," Chelley added with a little squeeze. "I still like you better than any horse. But it sure is nice to have a friend to play with." As she stroked the rabbit's soft fur, she thought about Morey. "I'd never let anyone throw you out a window. Even if it meant not having any friends."

On the morning of the big egg drop, the classroom was buzzing louder than normal. Chelley tried not to notice Chris and Steven as they whispered and laughed and looked at the hamster cage. *I should tell Mrs. Yount. She would stop them,* Chelley thought. But she knew she wouldn't.

"I'll be waiting down below," Mrs. Yount said at science time. "One member of each team should come with me." Once she was on the ground, Mrs. Yount began to call names. "Andrea. You're first." Andrea tossed a big roll of paper towels out the window. The egg inside the tube didn't break. "Very good," Mrs. Yount called. "Chelley!"

As Chelley turned to pick up the basketball, she saw Chris reach into the hamster cage and pull Morey out. The parachute was in his other hand.

"Stop it!" Chelley shouted. Out loud. Chris froze. Chelley's face got red, but she said it anyway. "If you don't put him back, I'll tell Mrs. Yount right now."

"Aw, come on," Chris started to say. "It's not going to hurt you."

"But it might hurt Morey," Chelley said. "Play your stupid tricks some other way." From the window, they could hear Mrs. Yount calling for Chelley. Chelley just stared at Chris until he put the hamster back into the cage.

Then she leaned out the window and tossed the basketball toward Caitlin. It thudded on the ground, and Caitlin raced over to open it up. "It worked!" she shouted, holding up the unbroken egg. Chelley waved, then stepped back. Without

looking at the faces of the other kids, she went and sat at her desk.

By lunchtime, everyone had heard about what Chelley had done. "You really forced Chris to put the hamster back?" Caitlin asked. "You're braver than I am."

"No, I'm not," Chelley said. "I just couldn't let him hurt Morey." As she talked, Andrea walked up to their table.

"Hi! Can I sit with you guys?" she asked. Sitting beside Caitlin, she looked across at Chelley. "I'm glad you stopped Chris and Steven this morning. I didn't want them to do it either, but I didn't think I could stop them."

Chelley almost choked on her milk. "Thanks."

"And don't worry about them pulling tricks on you. We'll keep our eyes open. Right, Caitlin?"

"Right," Caitlin agreed. "Friends stick together." She held up her milk carton. So did Andrea. "Right, Chelley?"

Chelley's face got a little red, but she lifted her carton. "Right."

My Friend Fang

13

"Grrrr."

Rachel was halfway across her yard, headed toward the car where her mother sat waiting. But that sound told her that the Thomsens' big dog, Fang, was in her yard. And she was afraid.

"Come on, Rachel," her mom called.

Rachel twisted her head around and saw the big black dog's mean eyes staring right at her. And she saw his big teeth.

Closing her eyes, Rachel took a deep breath, then turned and ran for her life. Sure that the dog's teeth were right behind her, she jerked the car door open and jumped in.

"Rachel, why are you so afraid of dogs? You've never been bitten by one," Mom asked as Rachel buckled her seat belt.

"I don't know. They have such big teeth. I get scared just thinking about them." Rachel shivered as she talked.

At school that day, Rachel's teacher made an announce-

Dealing with fear; fear of dogs

ment. "Our local police department is asking for our help. Sometimes, when there is an emergency, like a fire or car accident, children get hurt or scared. If you have any stuffed animals that you don't play with anymore, but are still good, you might like to donate them for the officers to give away to those children."

Rachel's friend Amy raised her hand. "Mrs. Anderson, can we collect more animals from other people?"

"Yes, you can, Amy. The police department sent us these information letters in case anyone wanted to ask people in their neighborhood to donate animals also."

Amy whispered to Caroline and Rachel, "Let's ask our mothers if we can go collecting stuffed animals together after school."

Their mothers agreed that it was a good idea. "They can start in our neighborhood tomorrow," Rachel's mother said. "I'll be home then in case they need any help."

Rachel had only taken two steps out of the car the next afternoon when she remembered something. *Fang! What if he's out today?* When she stopped moving, Amy and Caroline stopped too.

"What's wrong, Rachel?" Caroline asked. "Did we forget something?"

Rachel shook her head and looked up the street.

"You changed your mind and now you don't want to ask for animals?" Amy guessed.

"I want to," Rachel answered as she turned and looked down the street. "I just don't want to go out in my neighborhood."

"Are your neighbors the mean kind?" Caroline asked.

"No, no. At least, not the people," Rachel answered.

"Well, what is it?" Amy almost exploded. "Your neighborhood has been attacked by aliens? Or wild animals? What? You keep looking around like you're afraid of something."

Rachel hung her head. "The Thomsens have a big black dog named Fang. I'm watching out for him because he scares me."

Caroline looked around. She seemed a little frightened too. "How big is he?" she asked in a whispery voice.

Amy shook her head. "My mother taught me how to deal with dogs. Come on." They started down the street. "You have to know that dogs always try to find out who's the toughest— who's dominant—when they meet. That's why you see them stare at each other and growl and show their teeth."

"Fang has big teeth," Rachel said with a shiver.

Amy went on. "Whenever you walk into a dog's yard, he sees you as a threat to his property. A dog that's used to being the toughest wants to know if he's tougher than you. That's why you shouldn't lean over and look him in the eye and smile."

"But doesn't that show that you're friendly?" Caroline asked.

"Not to a dog," Amy said. "To him, you're doing everything but growling to prove that you are tougher, more dominant. So he wants to prove his toughness by fighting."

"So what should I do if a big dog runs at me?" Rachel asked.

"Just stand still. Don't run, don't scream, just stand still and straight. Let the dog come to you. Maybe talk to it quietly, but let him decide that he is the toughest and you are no threat to him."

"Then he'll go away?"

"He'll walk away, and you can back slowly out of his yard. If he runs at you again, just freeze again." Amy smiled at her friends. "It's not that bad. You get used to dealing with dogs after a while. And only a few are really mean."

The girls began knocking on doors, and the people were happy to help. Soon, they had more stuffed animals than they could carry. "Whoa! Help!" Amy shouted as she slipped. Six teddy bears hit the sidewalk.

"Here." Rachel laughed. "Baby-sit my four monkeys, and I'll go to the next house." She was almost to the door when she heard the growl.

There was Fang, right at the corner of the house, staring straight at her. Rachel froze. All she could see was Fang's big teeth.

My Friend Fang

It was too late to run. Rachel tried to remember what Amy had said. *Cover my eyes? Turn my back? Scream at the top of my lungs? No, now I remember. I hope she was right.*

Standing straight up, she watched out of the corner of her eyes as the dog walked up to her, still growling and showing his teeth. She even tried to talk to him. "That's a good boy, Fang." Fang stopped growling and looked confused.

Out on the sidewalk, Amy and Caroline held their breath. Just then, the door of the house flew open. "Fang, come here. Leave that poor girl alone!" It was Mrs. Thomsen. Immediately, Fang ran to her. "I'm sorry, Rachel."

Rachel started breathing again. She tried to smile. Mrs. Thomsen went on. "Come on in. And bring your friends. Fang, you should be ashamed for being mean to these nice girls."

Fang did look ashamed. He crawled along the floor and tried to cover his sad eyes with his paws. Rachel almost felt sorry for him. "Why, he's just a big puppy," she said.

"Just a big baby," Mrs. Thomsen agreed. "Fang, I want you to be friends with Rachel. Come here." Fang jumped up and walked over to Rachel and Mrs. Thomsen. "Now, Fang, shake hands and say you're sorry. Rachel, put your hand out."

Rachel hesitated, but she put her hand out toward Fang and his teeth. Fang raised his paw, and they shook. Then he opened his mouth and . . . licked her hand twice. "Now, you'll be friends," Mrs. Thomsen said.

Rachel petted Fang while her friends explained about the stuffed animals. The dog looked up at her and showed his teeth. "Look," she said, "I think Fang is smiling at me!"

Great Stories for Kids

Your children will love the adventures and drama of the five-volume set *Great Stories for Kids,* and you'll value the character-building lessons they learn while reading these treasured stories. Each volume is bound in durable hardcover with delightful color illustrations. Also available in Spanish and French.

The Bible Story

The Bible Story was written not just to tell the wonderful stories in the Bible, but each story was especially written to teach your child a different character-building lesson—lessons such as honesty, respect for parents, obedien kindness, and many more. This is truly the pleasant way to influence your child's character. The set contains more than 400 stories spread over 10 volumes. Hardcover.

Uncle Arthur's Bedtime Stories

For years this collection of stories has been the center of cozy reading experiences between parents and children. Arthur Maxwell tells the real-life adventures of young children—adventures that teach the importance of character traits such as kindness and honesty. Five volumes, hardcover.

Quigley's Village (video series for kids)

Quigley's videos, for ages 2-7, teach children biblical va ues through the adventures of Mr. Quigley and his loveabl puppet friends. They are filled with stories, songs, humor, and fun, helping children to learn and grow. Perfect for teaching values at home, school, or church. They are approximately 30 minutes in length.

For more information, mail the postpaid card, or write to: Pacific Press Marketing Service, P.O. Box 5353, Nampa, ID 83653.